D0403753

Happy Holi-Doodles!

Written by Michael Joosten
Based on a television script by Karen Moonah
Illustrated by Christopher Moroney

A GOLDEN BOOK · NEW YORK

Happy holidays! Here you can draw, color, and complete the scenes. Let's go, go, go!

Help the Cat in the Hat decorate for his Christmas celebration.

Will you draw a path so everyone can get to the Cat in the Hat's Christmas party?

Can you fill the table with yummy food?

Will you draw whiskers on Fifi the Mouse?

Draw wings on the penguins!

Will you draw ropes for the monkeys to swing on?

Who is the Cat in the Hat greeting at the best Christmas party ever?

It's time for musical chairs! Can you draw three chairs so we can play?

Quick! Hide ten candy canes for the candy cane hunt!

Will you draw cups and stripy straws for Thing One and Thing Two?

Draw a starfish on Daphne the Dolphin's tail.

Will you make a hot dog for the anaconda to eat?

Who is the Cat in the Hat waving good-bye to?

The Cat in the Hat will need a broom to clean up after his party.
Draw the end of the broom.

The Cat in the Hat needs a tail!

Let's light up Sally's house with big and bright Christmas lights!

Brrr! It's cold! Can you draw warm scarves for Sally and Nick?

How many candy canes can you hang from Ralph's antlers?

The Cat in the Hat loves his umbrella.
Will you decorate it for Christmas?

It's time to decorate the gingerbread house!

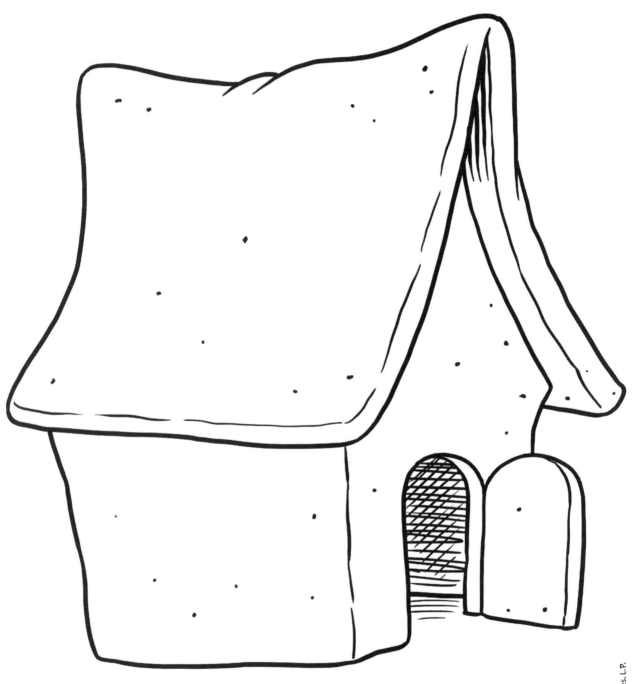

Fifi the Mouse is on top of the clock. Can you draw her there?

There is a very stinky animal at the Christmas party.
Draw what it is.

Can you draw a shell for this turtle?

Thing One and Thing Two need horns to honk!

Beavers need big front teeth to chomp on wood.
Will you draw teeth for them?

We made a big mess at the party.
Can you draw it so we can clean it up?

The Thinga-ma-jigger needs propellers to fly Nick and Sally home for Christmas.

We're decorating the Christmas tree. Will you help us?

Let's make snow angels!

We're building a snowman. Want to help us?

Thing One and Thing Two need snow boots.
Will you make a pair for each of them?

Ice-skate. You skate. We all love to ice-skate! Color it!

It's time to hang stockings from the fireplace!

We love to make footprints in the snow. Draw them!

Can you give Sally some mittens?

Nick's head will get cold without a hat!

The Cat in the Hat loves marshmallows in his hot chocolate.

WOO-HOO! Draw a sled for Thing One and Thing Two.

What kind of cookies should Nick and Sally leave out for Santa?

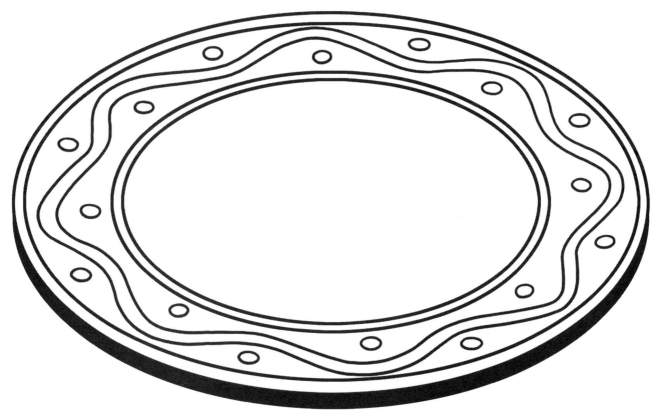

Let's feed chestnuts to the squirrels.

Draw what's on your Christmas list this year!

Can you design Sally's Christmas dress?

Can you decorate Nick's Christmas sweater?

We need a horse for our sleigh ride!

Draw a chimney for Santa to come down on Christmas.

Who is flying the Thinga-ma-jigger?

Nick and Sally made a Christmas ornament for the Cat in the Hat.
Can you make an ornament?

The Fish needs Christmas decorations for his bowl. Will you make some?

What are Sally and Nick jumping over?

Make a Christmas card for the Cat in the Hat!

Let's throw snowballs!

Can you help Thing One and Thing Two make a snow fort?

Let's put a star at the top of the Christmas tree!

Draw a present inside this box.

The Cat needs his hat!

Who is handing Nick and Sally a Christmas present?

Can you put wrapping paper and ribbons on these presents?

Can you draw snowflakes for everyone to catch?

Will you draw jingle bells for Thing One and Thing Two to shake?

The penguins need a pond to swim in. Draw it!

Draw the big red button that starts the Thinga-ma-jigger.

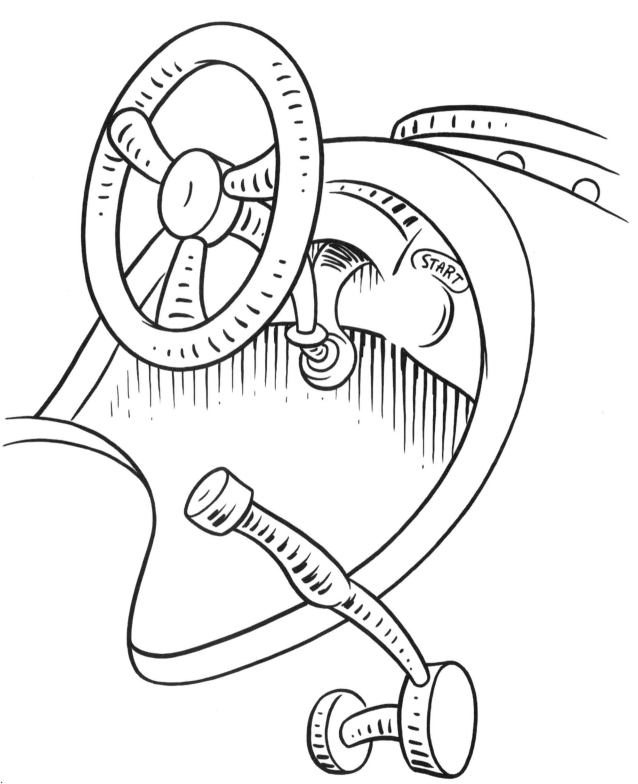

Ralph is sleeping. Can you draw him a blanket so he stays warm?

Look! Ralph is hiding behind the Christmas tree!

The Cat in the Hat is tangled in Christmas lights!
What colors are they?

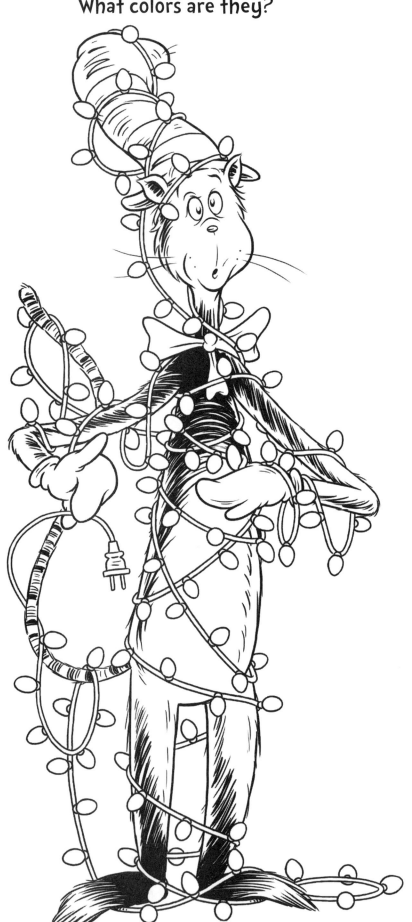

What kind of Christmas decorations are
Thing One and Thing Two holding?

If you could have any Christmas present you wanted, what would it be?
Draw it.

The Cat in the Hat needs skis! Can you draw him a pair?

Draw a map of Freeze-Your-Knees Snowland.

Can you draw a toolbox so we can fix the Thinga-ma-jigger?

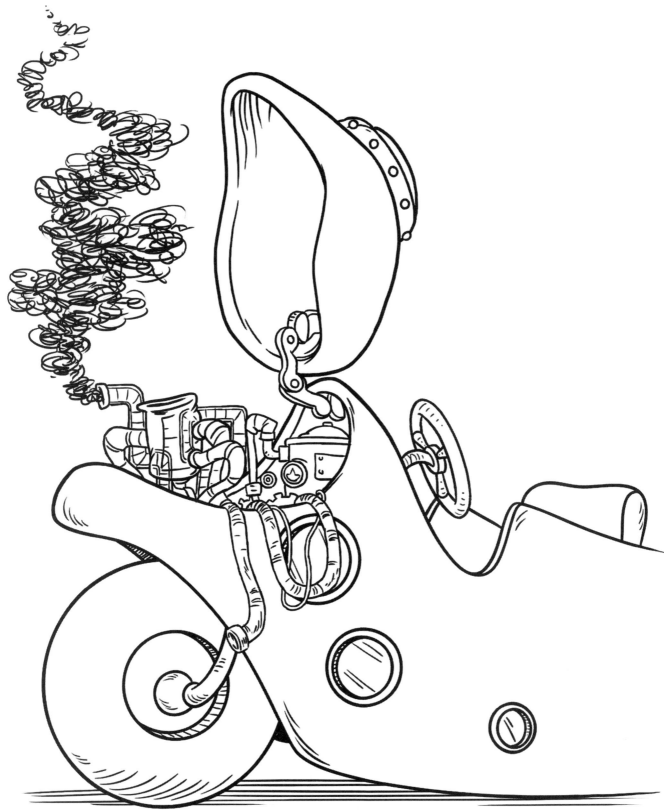

Ralph loves to eat plants. Will you draw him some?

The Thinga-ma-jigger needs ice cream cones so it can fly. Draw them!

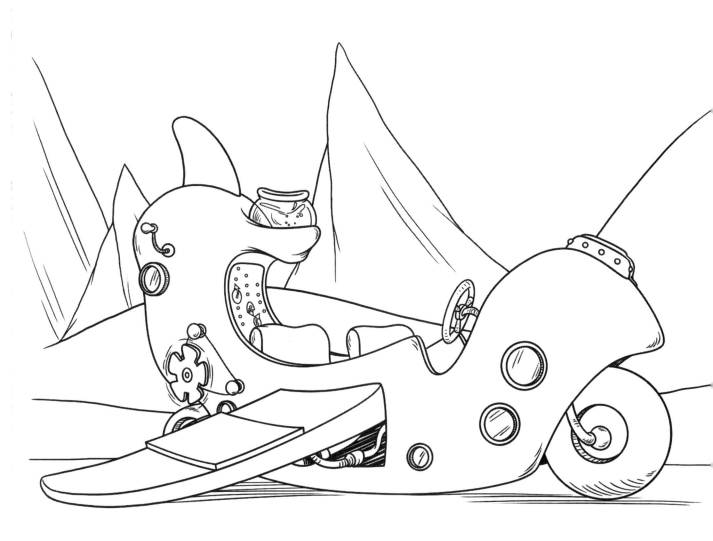

Draw tusks on Effia, Thimba, and Bisa.

Someone is hiding in the tall grass. Draw who it is.

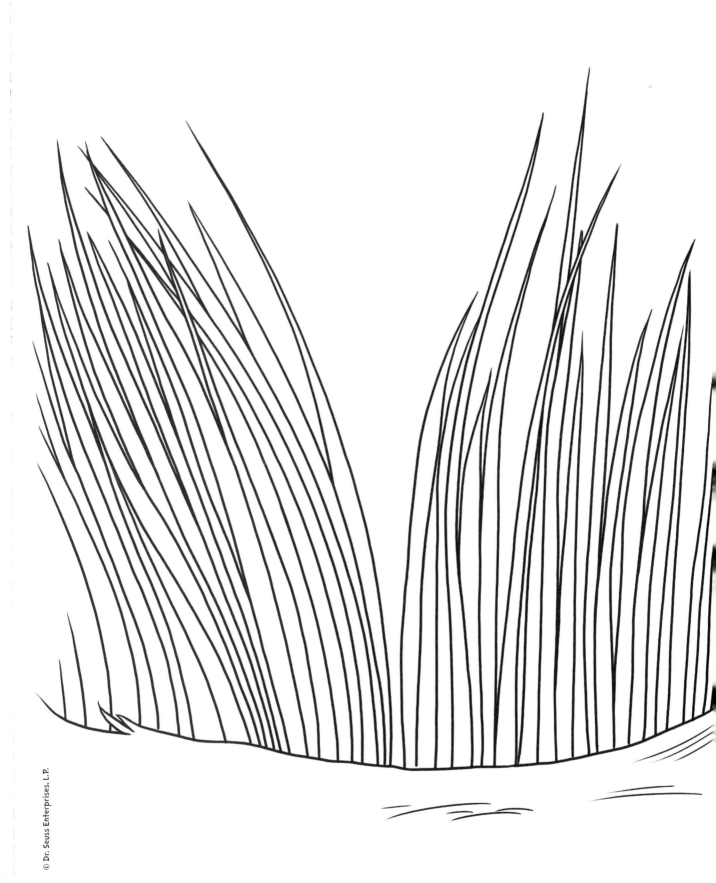

How many giant bugs can you draw on Ralph's antlers?

What type of fruit is hanging from the tree?

Look! There are hippos in the watering hole!
Draw them!

It's really hot in the savanna.
Will you draw some clouds to hide the sun?

Draw the Cat in the Hat riding Bisa.

Will you draw a trail so we can reach the watering hole?

Will you draw wheels on the Thinga-ma-jigger?

Will you draw a colorful sunset for us to watch?

Santa brought Sally a jump rope. Draw it.

Draw fruit on the fruitcake.

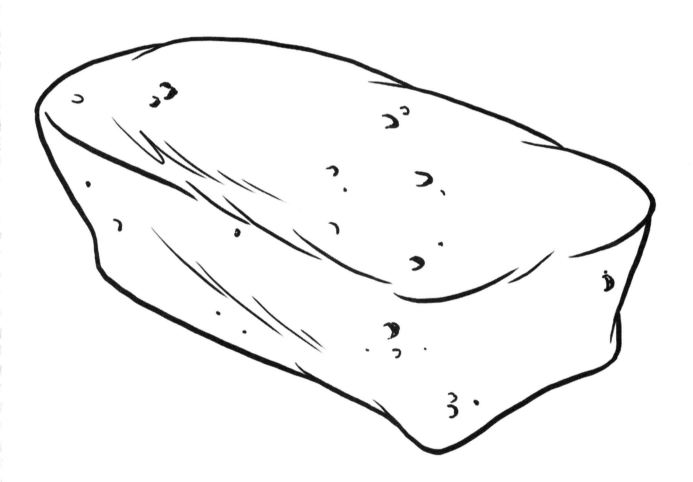

Will you draw Nick and Sally's tree house?

Can you draw antlers on Ralph's head?

Santa brought the Fish a tiny umbrella for his bowl. Will you draw it?

Draw Nick and Sally's footprints in the snow.

Let's eat snow cones with Thing One and Thing Two!

Who do you think Nick is carrying in the bowl?

Deck the Thinga-ma-jigger with boughs of holly.

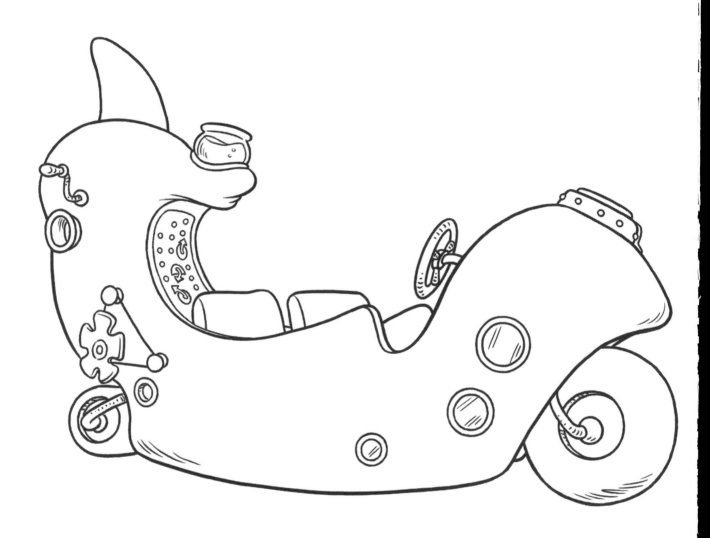

Can you draw Freeze-Your-Knees Snowland?

The snow is so bright that Thing One and Thing Two need sunglasses. Draw them!

Ralph is so happy to see his parents! Draw a big smile on his face.

Santa needs his sleigh for Christmas. Will you make him one?

Ralph and his parents need harnesses so they can help Santa's sleigh fly. Draw them!

The Cat in the Hat needs to know what time it is.
Will you draw numbers on the clock for him?

The Fish is inside the snow globe. Draw him!

Draw more music notes so everyone can go caroling.

What is your favorite thing to do when it snows? Draw it!

We're trying to fix the Radia-toozle in the Thinga-ma-jigger.
Can you draw what it looks like?

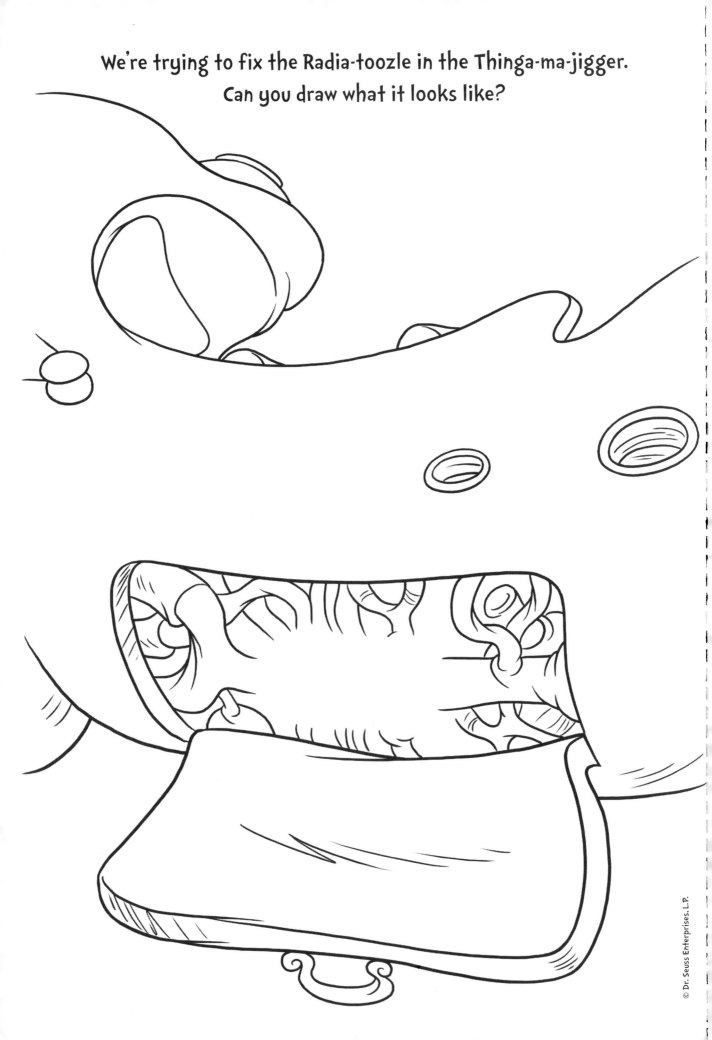

The Cat in the Hat is taking Nick and Sally to play hockey.
Draw them a puck and hockey sticks.

Draw a hoop for Daphne the Dolphin to jump through!

Snow is blocking Sally's front door!
Draw her a shovel so she can move it.

Decorate this Christmas wreath!

Can you draw claws on Mervin the Crab?

The Cat in the Hat is missing his bow tie! Draw him one.

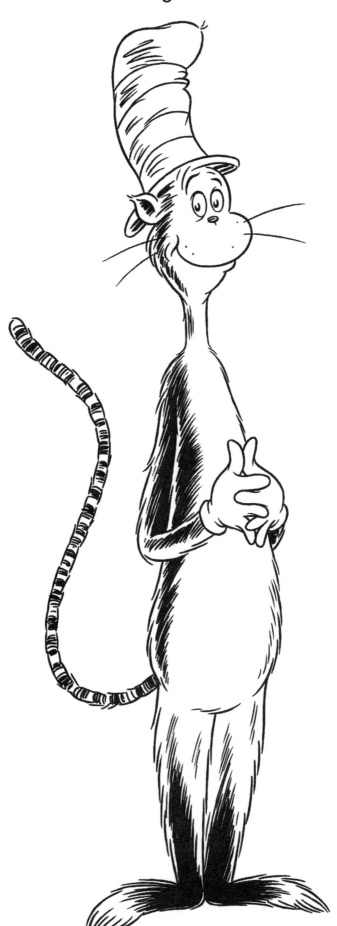

Can you draw Sally a headband?

Thing One and Thing Two are missing the numbers from their outfits. Can you write the numbers in?

Sally and Nick need some more popcorn on the string.
Can you draw some?

Draw your own super-duper-special Christmas picture here.

We want to spend Christmas at your house.
Will you draw it for us?

Will you draw Santa hats on Sally and Nick?

Can you decorate snowboards for Thing One and Thing Two?

Decorate Sally and Nick's Christmas pajamas.

The Cat in the Hat pulled something amazing out of his Christmas stocking. What is it?

Draw yourself with the Cat in the Hat.

Sally and Nick need their earmuffs. Will you draw them each a pair?

Let's decorate these Christmas cookies!

Sally wants to open her presents. Will you draw her a staircase?

Nick got a new basketball from Santa! Color it!

Look what Thing One and Thing Two got for Christmas!

What did the Fish get for Christmas?

It's time for Nick and Sally to hang their Christmas stockings on the mantel.

Let's put some presents under the tree!

Surprise! What Christmas gift would you give the Cat in the Hat?

You have completed the whole doodle book!
Celebrate by decorating the festive banner! Aren't you clever?